Don't miss any of the titles

in the ALIEN INVADERS series:

ROCKHEAD: THE LIVING MOUNTAIN

INFERNOX: THE FIRESTARTER

ZILLAH: THE FANGED PREDATOR

HYDRONIX: DESTROYER OF THE DEEP

ATOMIC: THE RADIOACTIVE BOMB

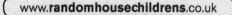

www.randomhousechildrens.co.uk

ALIEN INVADERS: INFERNOX, THE FIRESTARTER
A RED FOX BOOK 978 1 849 41231 5

First published in Great Britain by Red Fox,
an imprint of Random House Children's Publishers UK
A Random House Group Company

This edition published 2011

3 5 7 9 10 8 6 4 2

Set in Century Schoolbook

Red Fox Books are published by
Random House Children's Publishers UK, 61–63 Uxbridge Road, London W5 5SA

www.**randomhousechildrens**.co.uk
www.**randomhouse**.co.uk

Addresses for companies within The Random House Group Limited can be
found at: www.randomhouse.co.uk/offices.htm

THE RANDOM HOUSE GROUP Limited Reg. No. 954009

A CIP catalogue record for this book is available from
the British Library.

Penguin Random House is committed to a sustainable future for
our business, our readers and our planet. This book is made from
Forest Stewardship Council® certified paper.

MIX
Paper from
responsible sources
FSC® C018179

Printed and bound in Great Britain by Clays Ltd, St Ives plc

ALIEN INVADERS

MAX SILVER

INFERNOX
THE FIRESTARTER

RED FOX

THE GALAXY

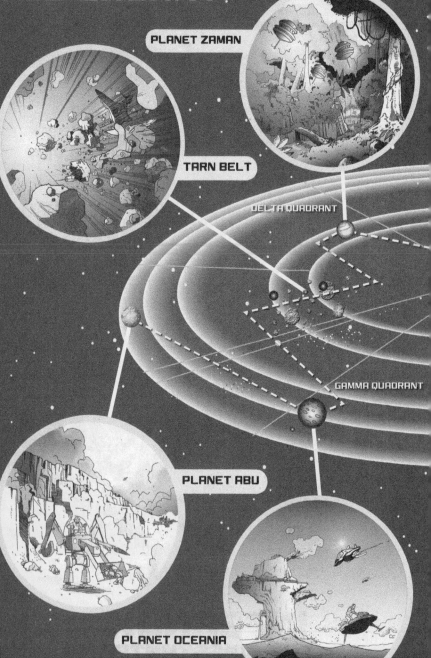

PLANET ZAMAN

TARN BELT

DELTA QUADRANT

GAMMA QUADRANT

PLANET ABU

PLANET OCEANIA

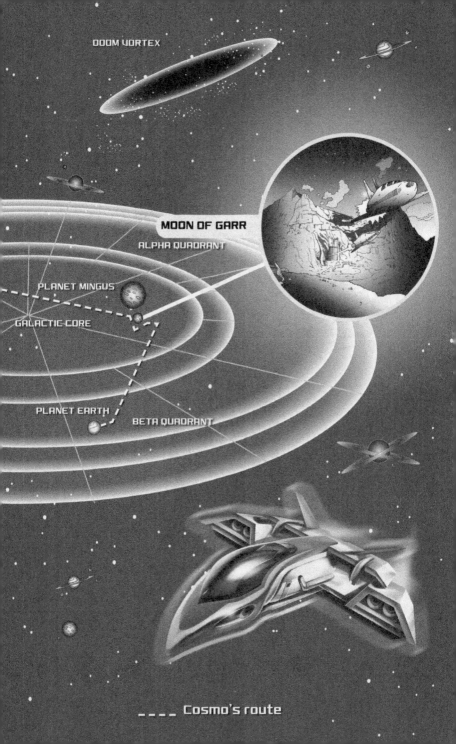

DOOM VORTEX

MOON OF GARR

ALPHA QUADRANT

PLANET MINGUS

GALACTIC CORE

PLANET EARTH

BETA QUADRANT

_ _ _ _ Cosmo's route

ATTENTION, ALL EARTHLINGS!

MY NAME IS G1 AND I AM CHIEF OF THE GALAXY'S SECURITY FORCE, G-WATCH. I BRING YOU GRAVE NEWS.

IT IS THE YEAR 2121, AND OUR PLANETS ARE UNDER ATTACK FROM THE OUTLAW KAOS. HE IS BEAMING FIVE ALIEN INVADERS INTO THE GALAXY, COMMANDING THEM TO DESTROY IT. IF THEY SUCCEED, THIS WILL BE THE END OF US ALL.

A HERO MUST BE FOUND TO SAVE US: ONE WHO WILL VENTURE THROUGH THE TREACHEROUS REGIONS OF SPACE; ONE WITH AN UNCOMMON COURAGE WITH WHICH TO FIGHT THESE INVADERS; ONE WHO POSSESSES THE POWER OF THE UNIVERSE! THAT HERO IS AN EARTHLING BOY. HE IS OUR ONLY HOPE.

INVADER ALERT!

In the wild jungle of Planet Zaman, robot
DEL-8 rolled between the trees on its
caterpillar tracks, its forklift arms
carrying a crate of sparkling berries. It
trundled into a large clearing where
Planet Zaman's only building stood –
the Eco-Tec Medicines Laboratory. The
delivery-bot swivelled its camera eye,
blinking in the lilac sunlight, then rolled
in through the laboratory door.

"Starberries for sorting," it announced through its voicebox.

Inside, hundreds more robots were at work, creating advanced galactic medicines from the plants that grew in the jungles of Zaman. Robot DEL-8 tipped the crate of starberries out onto a conveyor belt, where a team of sorting-bots began removing the berries' stalks with their pincers and cleaning them with electric brushes.

DEL-8 selected a tray of the juiciest berries and took them over to the processing area, where processor-bots were waiting, piston arms raised.

"Juicy starberries for pulping," DEL-8 said, placing the tray on a workbench.

The processor-bots squashed the berries to a pulp, then extractor-bots rolled in and sucked up the paste with their hoses, sending it into their mixing tanks. There was a whirr as they separated the chemicals, then squirted a sticky syrup into jars. The team of robots were preparing starberry syrup, one of the most precious medicines in the galaxy. It was the only cure for comet cough, a terrible illness carried in the toxic vapour trails of comets. Packager-bots packed the jars of syrup into boxes, ready to be collected by cargo ships and distributed to the galaxy's planets.

All through the laboratory, teams of robots were busy turning jungle plants into medicines: glimpan-tree wax for sun blisters, zinger-pollen spray for gravity sickness, mistlemoss cream for dongaloids, oozing-buckthorn ointment for tentacle tension, and even nut-nectar bug-eye drops.

Robot DEL-8 rolled out of the door to fetch another crate. But as it headed into the jungle, a loud roar sounded overhead. Its camera eye swivelled, glancing up through the trees. Its circuits whirred, puzzled by what it saw: a huge ball of fire was hurtling down through the sky.

DEL-8's processor calculated that the fireball was heading straight for the laboratory. It bleeped in alarm: "Danger! Danger!"

Suddenly the huge ball of fire smashed down onto the building. In a massive explosion, robots, machinery and medicines were blasted in all directions. DEL-8 was sent flying backwards, smashing into a tree trunk.

"Emergency!" it called, crashing to the ground. It tried to right itself, but its caterpillar tracks had jammed. Its camera eye focused on the burning laboratory. "Emergency!"

Flames raged through the building and thick black smoke rose high into the sky. Then out of the flames stepped an enormous alien creature.

DEL-8 bleeped fearfully, seeing the alien grinning. "Intruder! Intruder!"

The alien glowed red-hot and towered even higher than the burning laboratory. He roared menacingly, spewing fire from his mouth like a volcano.

"I am Infernox, and by order of Kaos I've come to set this planet ablaze!"

CHAPTER
ONE

THE MISSION

"Destination: Planet Zaman!" Cosmo said,
blasting the Dragster 7000 spaceship
away from Garr. "Point me in the right
direction, Nuri."

"Programming route co-ordinates now,"
his co-pilot, Agent Nuri, replied. She was
tapping numbers into the spaceship's
navigation console, a look of concentration
on her blue-skinned face. "Done," she said.
She tapped the spacescreen, activating its

star plotter, and words lit up on the glass:

DESTINATION: PLANET ZAMAN
STAR SYSTEM: DYAD-24
ROUTE: HYPERWAY 55 FROM THE BIG DIPPER CONSTELLATION
DISTANCE: 2.6 BILLION MILES

Cosmo felt excited. Through the spacescreen, in the distance, he could see a pattern of seven stars shaped like a

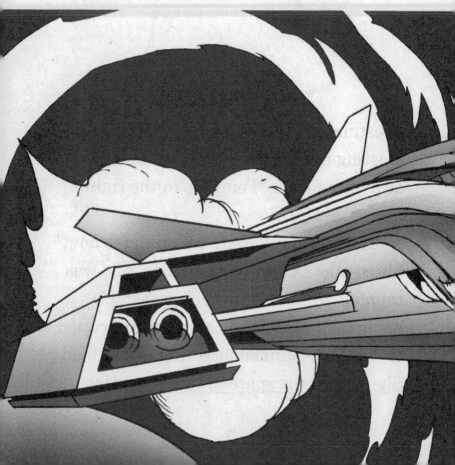

frying pan – the Big Dipper constellation.

"Are you ready for another adventure, Nuri?"

"I sure am, Cosmo!"

"Then it's full speed ahead!"

Cosmo nudged the steering column, turning towards the Big Dipper, and increased speed to eleven vectrons. They were on their way.

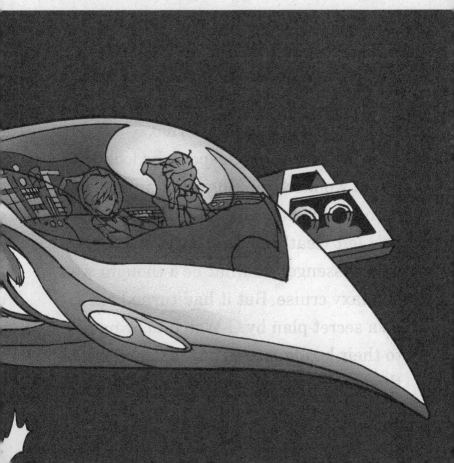

Cosmo Santos was an eleven-year-old Earthling boy on a mission for the galactic security force G-Watch to save the galaxy from five alien invaders. The invaders were being beamed in by the galactic outlaw Kaos, using navicom transportation devices, and were under orders to destroy the galaxy. So far, Cosmo had defeated the first of them – Rockhead, the living mountain – in a fierce battle on Garr. Now he was heading west to the jungle planet, Zaman, to face the second invader, the fire alien Infernox.

As he flew through space, he looked out in wonder, thinking what an amazing turn his life had taken. Only yesterday he'd left Heathrow Spaceport on Earth as a passenger on what he'd thought was a galaxy cruise. But it had turned out to be a secret plan by G-Watch to bring him to their headquarters on Garr, and from then on his whole life had changed.

Cosmo had discovered that he was unique. Inside him was a power – the power of the universe – which was present in all living things but unusually strong in Cosmo. It gave him courage and a lightning-like energy when facing danger. Cosmo's father had been the first to notice it in him when he was very young. Cosmo dipped the Dragster's fins, shooting through the stars of the Big Dipper. *If only you could see me now, Dad*, he thought. *I'm a G-Watch agent!* Cosmo's dad had been a G-Watch agent too, but had died two years ago in a space-crash. Cosmo still thought about him every single day.

Up ahead, the flashing lights of space beacons marked the entry to Hyperway 55, one of the galaxy's high-speed space lanes. Cosmo wove the Dragster between them then opened a panel on its steering column, revealing a silver switch.

"Engaging hyperdrive, Nuri," he said.

Cosmo flicked the switch and was thrust back into his seat by the force of the acceleration. The stars in the spacescreen turned to bright white streaks as the Dragster 7000 shot across the galaxy at hyperspeed, twice the speed of light.

"Are you ready to face the enemy, Cosmo?" Nuri asked.

"I think so," Cosmo replied, a little apprehensively.

"You can do it! Trust in your power, Cosmo," Nuri told him. "You'll be great – just like you were against Rockhead. And I'll be looking out for you too. We're a team, remember."

Cosmo remembered how he had beaten the first alien by transforming into Mucosa the slugoid. *Well, there's no turning back now*, he thought. As he blasted along the hyperway, a feeling of courage began to well up inside him, and his spacesuit glowed. He was wearing G-Watch's most advanced piece of technology – the Quantum Mutation Suit, a living body armour infused with particles from the beginning of the universe. Activated by the power inside him, it enabled Cosmo to mutate into alien forms to fight any opponent.

"We're nearly there," Nuri said. "Exit hyperway in seven seconds."

"Already?" Cosmo asked. "That was two-point-six billion miles? Wow, hyperspeed is fast!"

"... *four* ... *three* ... *two* ... *one* ..."

Cosmo flicked the hyperdrive switch back and turned the steering column. His ears popped as the spaceship veered off the hyperway then slowed to seven vectrons. Through the spacescreen he saw two enormous stars orbited by a cluster of vibrantly coloured planets.

"Welcome to the Dyad-24 star system," Nuri said. She tapped the screen, activating its star plotter, and words lit up on the glass beside each astral object.

PLANET UMAX ... PLANET OBON ... PLANET JUNOK ... PLANET ZAMAN! Cosmo read, seeing a large green planet straight ahead. He powered the Dragster towards it, slowing to two vectrons as they entered the planet's atmosphere. He switched the spaceship to planetary mode, and the

14

cabin pressure self-adjusted as the ship flew into a lilac sky. Cosmo looked down and saw a vast jungle of trees veined with silver rivers. It was incredible – far bigger than any jungle on Earth. From his vantage point in the Dragster he could see the trees covering hills and valleys as far as the horizon.

"Zaman's jungle contains some of the most incredible plants in the universe," Nuri said. "It's where many of the galaxy's medicines originate from."

Cosmo took the Dragster low over the treetops to take a closer look. Some of the trees were enormous, and he saw alien creatures too: a herd of horned beasts grazing in a clearing; a flock of four-winged parrots flying alongside the Dragster. It was truly wild! He zigzagged along a winding river, then burst through the spray from a colossal waterfall.

Nuri checked the navigation console.
"G-Watch's scanners plotted the invader's
trajectory, and calculated that it would
have struck around here. Keep an eye out."

Cosmo peered down apprehensively.
Where are you, Infernox? he thought.

Nuri reached across the control desk
and gently tapped a bug-like robot.
"Brain-E, wake up – we've arrived."

Brain-E, the ship's brainbot, bleeped and

its lights came on. "Good day, Miss Nuri."

"I've never known a robot sleep as much as you do, Brain-E," Nuri laughed. "Tell us what you know about the alien invader Infernox."

The little robot stretched its six metal legs, then bleeped again, searching its databank. "According to my data, Infernox is an alien of volcanic origin from an ever-expanding sun in the Doom Vortex."

Cosmo gulped. He knew from his encounter with the first alien, Rockhead, how powerful aliens from the distant Doom Vortex could be.

"Infernox is a firestarter," the brainbot continued. "And can emit immense heat in the form of fireballs."

"Fireballs in a medicine jungle! That doesn't sound good!" Cosmo said. He peered over the trees and saw a column of smoke rising into the sky. "I think I've spotted where he struck. There's a fire over there!"

He looked down. Below, a building in a clearing was ablaze. Cosmo flew closer, looking anxiously to see if Infernox was still around, but thick black smoke was pouring into the sky and fierce flames raged thirty metres high. "I can't see properly. There's too much smoke," he said.

Nuri gasped. "The fire's out of control."

"We have to put it out before it spreads to the jungle," Cosmo told her.

Nuri went to check the kit shelves at the back of the cockpit. "We've only got a handheld flame-freezer, Cosmo," she said, grabbing a gun-like gadget. "It's designed for putting out engine fires, not huge fires like that. Those flames are too big!"

Cosmo banked the Dragster and circled above the burning building, desperately wondering what to do. The flames leaped around the spacescreen, the spaceship's engines making the air swirl violently.

"Careful, Cosmo," Nuri said. "You're pulling the flames towards us!"

That gave Cosmo an idea. *A crazy idea. But it might just work*, he thought. He pulled back the throttle, increasing the Dragster's speed. "Hold on tight, Nuri!"

"Cosmo, why are you accelerating?" she asked, alarmed.

"I'm going to make a whirlwind and try to suck these flames into the air," Cosmo replied, his heart racing. "I'm going to use the Dragster to put out the fire!"

CHAPTER TWO

A CRAZY PLAN

Cosmo fired the thrusters, sending the Dragster 7000 around in circles above the burning building. The speedometer crept upwards – *two vectrons . . . three vectrons . . . four vectrons* – the force pushing Cosmo and Nuri back into their seats. Cosmo tilted the Dragster on its side so that its top touched the edge of the blaze.

"I feel dizzy, Cosmo," Nuri said, her blue Etrusian skin tinged with green, as if she was going to be sick.

"Me too!" said Brain-E. The little brainbot had clasped its legs around the navigation console on the control desk and was desperately trying to hang on.

The Dragster was making the air whirl round and round, drawing the smoke and flames into a spiral.

Cosmo accelerated even more. *Five vectrons . . . six vectrons . . .* He gripped the steering column tightly, making sure the Dragster didn't dip too low and crash into the jungle. The Dragster spun faster and faster, until Cosmo felt as if his stomach was rising up into his chest. He could hardly see through the spacescreen; it was a blur of smoke and fire and trees.

"Please slow down, Master Cosmo, my circuits aren't built for this," Brain-E called from the control desk.

The column of smoke and flames swirled faster, forming a burning whirlwind above the building. Cosmo steadily took the Dragster higher, circling faster still, and the flames rose with it. He was sucking the flames up out of the building, lifting them high into the sky.

"It's working!" Nuri said.

For a moment the fire raged, whirling in mid air. But with nothing to feed on, the flames began to die down, flickering and burning themselves out.

Cosmo eased off the throttle as the fire cleared, slowing the Dragster. His head was spinning. "Is everyone OK?" he asked.

Nuri had slid off her chair and Brain-E was dangling by one leg from the control desk. "My circuits feel peculiar," the brainbot spluttered.

Nuri pulled herself up, her face green but smiling. "Nice job, Cosmo!" she said.

Cosmo looked down, relieved to see that the fire was out, though the building was charred and black. "I can't see Infernox," he said. "Come on, let's go down and check the place out."

He reduced power to the Dragster's thrusters and descended, touching down beside the building on a scorched patch of ground. As he switched off the spaceship's engine, Nuri checked the external gauges.

"Temperature outside is thirty-six degrees centigrade," she said. "Gravity normal. Oxygen level plentiful."

Cosmo and Nuri both stood up and headed for the cockpit door. Cosmo pressed the exit release button and the door slid open. He felt warm air on his face and heard the hoots and caws of alien creatures coming from the jungle. He stepped down onto the burned ground, feeling a mixture of nerves and excitement; Zaman was only the second alien planet he'd visited.

"Master Cosmo, wait for me," Brain-E called, scuttling after him.

"Be careful, everyone," Nuri said. "Infernox could be nearby." She had the flame-freezer in one hand; with the other she took a phaser gun from her utility belt and held it ready in case the alien invader was waiting to ambush them.

Cosmo's heart was pounding as he crept towards the blackened shell of the building. "What is this place?" he whispered. "It's ruined."

Brain-E followed, picking its way carefully along the hot ground. "According to my databank, Master Cosmo, this was the Eco-Tec Medicines Laboratory," the brainbot said. "It's where galactic medicines are made."

The charred remains of dozens of robots lay on the ground, their circuit boards blown open and their casings melted. Brain-E went over to one and examined it. "Its circuits are frazzled."

Nuri leaned down to see. "Caused by an explosion," she whispered.

Cosmo cautiously stepped inside the burned-out laboratory, his spaceboots crunching on hot ash and broken glass. The laboratory's walls were torn open and blackened, conveyor belts lay twisted and broken, and more charred robots littered the floor. He went over to inspect a large black crater. "Look at this, Nuri."

She peered in. "It's an impact crater," she said. Then she glanced up: most of the roof had caved in. "Infernox definitely beamed down here. He must be huge!"

"So where is he now?" Cosmo said. He headed back outside and looked around into the jungle. Suddenly he heard a *blip-bloop* from under a tree, and saw an upturned robot with forklift arms trying to right itself. "Intruder," its voicebox said weakly. "Bot DEL-8 reporting emergency. Intruder! Intruder!"

Cosmo rushed over to the robot and knelt down beside it. "Are you OK?" He saw that its caterpillar tracks had melted and its control panel was sparking.

The robot tried to swivel its camera eye to look at Cosmo but the mechanism was jammed. "Intruder alert," it said weakly.

"Did you see the intruder?" Cosmo asked it.

"Affirmative," DEL-8 replied.

"Which way did he go?"

The robot raised a forklift arm, pointing into the jungle. "Intruder went north." But the effort was too much for it. There was a sizzling sound, and wisps of smoke rose from its control panel.

Cosmo heaved it upright, and battery acid leaked out.

"Systems faaaailinggg-g," the delivery-bot said, its voicebox melting. "Bot DEL-8 make no more deliveries noooooooow." The light in its camera eye went out.

"No!" Cosmo said desperately, inspecting DEL-8 for any trace of life. But its wires were severed and its circuit board was blown. *This little robot's shut down for good*, he thought sadly. He wiped the soot from its control panel, then glanced back at the laboratory. "Brain-E, Nuri, come here quickly."

They rushed over to join him.

"This one's only just shut down," Cosmo told them. "It saw Infernox. It said he went north into the jungle."

"But the jungle's massive," Nuri said. "He could have gone anywhere."

Brain-E examined the delivery-bot's circuitry, inserting a probe arm into its control panel and downloading the information from its databank. The little brainbot then projected a three-dimensional map of the jungle from its holographic imager. "Might this be of help, master?"

"Nice one, Brain-E," Cosmo said. A miniature jungle landscape shimmered in mid air, and he and Nuri scanned it for information. They saw the Eco-Tec Medicines Laboratory at its centre; further into the jungle dozens more locations marked where the medicinal plants grew.

"DEL-8 said Infernox went north,"

Cosmo said, tracing his finger
northwards from the laboratory through
the 3D jungle. He came to a golden tree
marked GLIMPAN. "What's this?"

Nuri looked worried. "It's a glimpan
tree," she said. "Glimpan-tree sap is the
cure for sun blisters."

Cosmo frowned. "Then we'd better
hurry before Infernox burns it down!"

CHAPTER THREE

TRACKING THE ALIEN

Cosmo set off into the jungle, with Nuri and Brain-E close beside, heading north towards the glimpan tree. Nuri held her phaser gun at the ready, and Brain-E scuttled along the leaf-littered ground, its scanners on full alert for the invader.

Cosmo looked up in awe. The trees towered above him, taller than any he'd seen on Earth, their branches fanning out like gigantic green umbrellas, with shafts of sunlight dappling their leaves. He saw a troop of alien monkeys swinging from vines. They looked different to Earth monkeys, with bright green fur and tails with hands. The jungle plants looked alien too: blue-leafed ferns, fluorescent tree mosses, and toadstools taller than he was. Alien flowers floated in the air, and he could smell their scents: peppermint, vanilla and cola.

"This place is incredible," he said.

Nuri stopped to examine a tree trunk. "Infernox has definitely come this way, Cosmo. This bark is burned."

Cosmo glanced left and right, keeping a lookout for the alien invader. A tall purple flower leaned down, puffing pollen in his face, and he jumped, startled. "There sure are some weird plants here," he said.

Brain-E bleeped. "Planet Zaman has one of the most diverse ecosystems in the whole galaxy, Master Cosmo. It has excellent soil, no winters and over thirty

hours of sunlight each day. It also has maximum humidity. It's the perfect climate for plants to prosper."

"But not for G-Watch agents – right, Cosmo?" Nuri smiled, wiping condensation from her visor.

"Don't worry about me," Cosmo laughed. He'd once been trekking in the jungle with his dad back on Earth and could handle the heat and humidity. He picked up the pace, ducking under tall arching tree roots and bouncing over spongy mosses.

They passed toadstools that glowed like electric lamps, and parted a curtain of hanging purple vines. They pushed through a thicket of giant waggling finger ferns, then waded across a sparkling stream, Cosmo carrying Brain-E. Nuri stopped on the far bank, kneeling to examine huge gouges in the wet mud.

"Something large has been this way," she said. "These are footprints."

"Infernox?" Cosmo asked.

"Brain-E, could you identify these please?" Nuri said.

The brainbot hurried over the muddy ground, extending its scanner arm. Shining a little laserlight, it measured the size and shape of the footprints, then ran the information through its databank. Its lights flashed as it searched for a match.

"These are the hoofprints of hogohons, Miss Nuri," it said. "Grazing beasts that roam in herds." From its holographic imager, Brain-E projected a small hologram of a three-horned beast that looked a bit like a dinosaur.

"We passed over a herd of those in the Dragster on the way in," Cosmo commented. "Are they dangerous?"

"They're best avoided," Brain-E told him. "They can be very territorial."

"Well, we have to keep going," Nuri said, and she pushed on northwards through the jungle, towards the glimpan tree.

Cosmo glanced around, checking that no hogohons were lurking in the thick undergrowth. He ducked under an enormous spider's web, and his arm brushed a fern crawling with orange ants. "Brain-E, are there any other dangers on Zaman?" he asked.

The brainbot's lights flashed and it projected a hologram of a thin yellow snake with two heads. "The most dangerous creature on Zaman is the twin-snake, Master Cosmo: a two-headed tree snake with powerful venom. Unless you have the antidote, one bite is fatal within twenty minutes."

Cosmo gulped nervously, carefully checking the trees for snakes. "So what's the antidote, Brain-E?"

"Yellowbell pollen," Brain-E replied.

Nuri glanced back. "Stay vigilant, you two, and keep up."

Cosmo clambered down a bank of gum palms, ducking beneath their low-hanging branches, then dashed through a swarm of buzzing yellow flies.

"Master Cosmo, I don't wish to alarm you," Brain-E said, "but my sensors are detecting smoke ahead of us."

Uh-oh, Cosmo thought. He sprinted past Nuri. "Nuri, hurry!"

As a breeze blew through the trees, Cosmo smelled the smoke himself. He heard the crackling of fire and ran into a clearing where a tall golden-leafed tree was ablaze. "It's the glimpan tree! We're too late, Nuri! Infernox has already been here!"

Nuri rushed to Cosmo's side and pointed the flame-freezer towards the flames. She pulled its trigger, sending out freezing cold pulses. The fire hissed and sputtered.

On the ground around the tree Cosmo saw more charred and frazzled robots. He rushed to see if any were still moving,

raising his hands to shield his face from the blaze.

"They're harvester-bots, Master Cosmo," Brain-E said, checking their circuit boards. "They care for the jungle plants."

They had heli-packs for flying, pincers for picking fruit, and hoses for watering, but all lay broken and burned.

Suddenly Cosmo heard a hooting cry from the glimpan tree. He looked up and saw a creature clinging to a branch, trying to escape the flames. It was about the size of a koala, but pink and slimy.

"Brain-E, there's an animal up there!" he cried.

Brain-E raised a telescopic eye. "It's a tree sloth, Master Cosmo. A young one. The poor thing is trapped."

"Then we've got to save it!"

CHAPTER FOUR

HELI-PACK RESCUE

Cosmo looked up at the helpless tree sloth, trying to think of a way to rescue it. *If I use the Quantum Mutation Suit, I could turn into a flying alien and fly up there*, he thought. He called to Nuri, who was still fighting the blaze with the flame-freezer. "Nuri, I'm going to mutate to save the tree sloth."

"No, Cosmo!" she shouted. "Mutating now will deplete your power. You need to save your strength for Infernox. I'll get these flames under control."

But the blaze was now burning even more intensely and was about to reach the tree sloth. Cosmo could hear it hooting for help. Thinking quickly, he reached down and began detaching the heli-pack from one of the burned-out harvester-bots. "Brain-E, do you think you can get this working again?" he asked.

"I should think so, Master Cosmo," the little brainbot said. It inserted two pincer arms into the heli-pack's control panel and touched two wires together. There was a spark, then its rotor blades began spinning. "Hold on tight," the brainbot said.

Cosmo held the heli-pack above his head. "Nuri, I'm going up," he called. "Keep battling the flames."

The rotor blades whirred, lifting Cosmo off the ground and carrying him up beyond the flames. He could feel the heat around him, and saw bubbling sap spitting from the tree's burning bark. He rose higher and reached out to the tree sloth. He gripped its slimy paw and it coiled its tail around his wrist.

"That's it. I'll get you out of here," Cosmo said.

"I'll clear you an exit route, Cosmo!" Nuri called.

Cosmo felt an icy blast and saw the flames subsiding around him, clearing the way down. The tree sloth was now safe in his grasp, but he didn't know how to get the heli-pack to take him down again.

"Hold on tight, little sloth!" He let go and dropped to the ground, landing in a heap as the heli-pack spun into the burning tree and exploded.

"Master Cosmo, are you OK?" Brain-E called, hurrying over.

Cosmo stood up, dusting himself down. The slimy tree sloth let go of his arm and hooted in gratitude. "I'm fine, Brain-E. The tree sloth is safe."

Brain-E extended a probe arm to check it, and the slimy sloth cuddled the little brainbot, covering it in pink slime. "Er . . . hello to you too," said Brain-E.

The sloth hooted once more, then, on all fours, padded slowly into the bushes.

Cosmo was glad that he'd saved the sloth, even if it was only one small creature. He glanced at Nuri, who was now bringing the blaze under control. "Will the glimpan tree survive?" he asked.

"Its bark is charred, and it's lost its leaves, but it will recover eventually," Nuri replied, sending out another blast from the flame-freezer, making sure the fire was completely extinguished. She clipped it onto her utility belt and wiped the sweat from her face.

Looking around at all the destruction – the blackened glimpan tree and the frazzled harvester-bots on the ground – Cosmo felt angry; his power welled up inside him. "We have to stop Infernox – fast," he said determinedly. "Before he destroys any more medicinal plants on the planet. Map please, Brain-E."

The brainbot switched on its holographic imager and projected the map of the jungle into the air.

Cosmo studied it. *Which way now?* he wondered. He saw all kinds of medicinal plantations to the northeast: a mistlemoss glade, rednut trees, ghostfungus, buckthorn bushes, and a grove of starberry trees along a riverbank.

Nuri looked at the map and gasped. "Oh my goodness, starberry trees!" she said. "If Infernox destroys those, thousands of galactic citizens will die – starberry syrup is the only cure for comet cough."

"Comet cough?"

"It's lethal, Cosmo. I had comet cough when I was little and nearly died. Starberry syrup is what saved me."

"Then we have to hurry," Cosmo said.

Nuri tapped a switch on her visor and it turned a dim red colour. "We'll use my visor's thermal imager to help detect him," she said, and they raced off through the trees.

CHAPTER FIVE

STAMPEDE

Far across the galaxy at G-Watch
headquarters on Garr, G1 – the Chief of
Galactic Security – paced to and fro in
the surveillance room. All satellite feeds
were down and no signals were coming in
from the Dyad-24 star system.

A bearlike alien, Agent Toki, was
operating the satellite switchboard with
his hairy clawed paw. "There's some kind
of jammer in operation, Chief."

"A jammer? It must be *him*," G1 replied.

At that moment the surveillance room's video wall flickered, and he saw an image of the five-headed alien, Kaos.

"It's no use, G1, I've blocked your signals," Kaos sneered. "I'm just saying hello, should you wish to surrender."

"Get off this frequency, Kaos," G1 said.

Kaos's five heads grinned, then his five noses twitched. "Oh dear, G1, I smell smoke in your galaxy. Oh yes, that's right – that crazed firestarter Infernox is carrying out my orders to destroy Zaman. Ha! You *LOSE*!"

G1 glared at Kaos with his silver eyes. "Withdraw the invader, Kaos."

"Now why would I want to do that?" Kaos asked him. "Infernox will soon burn all Zaman's precious medicines, and sickness and disease will spread throughout your galaxy. There will be plagues of gravity ulcers, solar boils

and moon measles – not to mention fatal comet cough. What will you do without your jungle medicines, G1? Billions will suffer and die, and the galaxy will beg me for mercy."

"Your invader will be stopped, Kaos,"
G1 said defiantly.

"Infernox will incinerate anyone
who gets in his way." Kaos's five heads
laughed, then the video wall flickered
and went blank.

"The signal's gone, Chief," Agent Toki
called from the switchboard.

G1 turned to look at him. "Get the
satellite feeds back up as quickly as
you can."

"Do you think the boy will be OK, Chief?"

"If anyone can defeat Infernox, the
Earthling can," G1 replied. "The power of
the universe is strong in him."

* * *

On Planet Zaman, Nuri led the way
northeast through the jungle, Cosmo
and Brain-E following close behind. With
her visor's thermal imager she could see
the heat trail that Infernox had left.

Cosmo noticed frazzled ferns and blackened bushes. He saw scorch marks on a fungi-ladder tree, the mushrooms on its trunk crispy and cooked. As they picked up the pace, scrambling their way through the jungle, he began to feel a little apprehensive. "Nuri, Infernox seems really powerful," he said.

"You can beat him, Cosmo," Nuri replied. "Trust in your power." She stopped beside a bush of orange berries. "Here – have one of these," she said. "You need to keep your strength up." She picked a berry and handed it to him. "These are multiberries. They grow on my home planet, Etrusia, too."

Cosmo suddenly realized how hungry he was. He hadn't eaten anything since his flight from Earth the day before! He chewed the multiberry and tasted all kinds of flavours: coconut . . . banana . . . strawberry . . . sausages . . .

Sausages? Cosmo thought. *Weird!* He kept chewing, and tasted chocolate, then apple pie.

Brain-E bleeped from beside the bush. "Multiberries contain all the goodness of a meal, Master Cosmo."

Cosmo could feel himself getting stronger. His courage was returning, and he leaped across a stream, determined to do his very best to defeat the invader.

Suddenly Nuri's pointy ears twitched. "I can hear something," she said.

"What is it?" Cosmo asked. Nuri's Etrusian hearing was superior to his own.

"I don't know. But there's something coming our way!"

Just then Cosmo felt the ground tremble. He heard roaring and rumbling, then branches snapping and birds squawking as they flew out of their nests up into the sky. He saw a curtain of vines part and a herd of large dinosaur-like creatures come charging through, heading straight for him and Nuri.

"Hogohons!" Nuri cried.

Brain-E leaped onto her arm, wrapping its legs around her like a wristwatch. "It's a stampede! Run!"

Cosmo and Nuri raced through a thicket of fangtail ferns, the hogohons charging behind, snorting and roaring.

"Faster – or we'll be trampled!" Nuri yelled, sweeping aside thorny leaves.

They sprinted down a slope, slipping and sliding on clumps of mucous moss. Cosmo glanced over his shoulder and saw the hogohons gaining, their hooves pounding like thunder.

"Why are they stampeding?" he yelled.

"Something must have spooked them," Nuri replied. "Just keep running!"

They raced into a grove of fungi-ladder trees, and Cosmo saw monkeys overhead, swinging through the branches,

screeching in panic. Parrots cawed and flew up out of the trees. All the jungle animals were in a frenzy.

The hogohon herd had almost caught up with them. "Up, Nuri!" Cosmo said, leaping into a fungi-ladder tree, using the mushrooms on its trunk as steps. Nuri raced up behind him, and they clung to a branch as the beasts charged past below.

"That was close," Nuri said, breathing heavily.

"Way too close," Cosmo agreed. He heard a whirring sound above his head and looked up, seeing harvester-bots buzzing upwards on their rotor-blades, fleeing the jungle.

Cosmo climbed higher so he could better see what was happening. The tree swayed as he pulled himself up from branch to branch. He must have been more than forty metres from the ground when he pushed his head out above the canopy and gazed around. To the northeast he saw smoke billowing into the sky. "Fires, Nuri!" he called. "The jungle creatures are spooked because there are fires." He counted twelve separate blazes. "Infernox has gone on a rampage!"

Nuri climbed up through the leaves with

Brain-E on her wrist, and saw fires and smoke everywhere. "We'll never put all those out with the flame-freezer," she said.

Cosmo took a deep breath. *If we don't stop Infernox soon*, he realized, *the entire jungle will burn.*

CHAPTER
SIX

A NASTY BITE

Cosmo and Nuri watched the harvester-bots whizzing up from the trees around them, trying to escape the blaze.

Brain-E bleeped to one and it stopped, hovering in mid air alongside them. Brain-E spoke to it in some kind of robot language, then sprang off Nuri's wrist into the air and took hold of the harvester-bot's picker arm; together they flew off.

"Where are you going?" Nuri called.

"You two get Infernox. Leave the jungle fires to me!" the brainbot called back.

Cosmo scanned the jungle looking for the invader, and to the northeast saw fresh flames raging as another fire took hold. "Nuri, one over there just started. Infernox must be that way."

"Oh no! Then he's nearly at the river where the starberry trees grow!"

Suddenly they heard a hideous roar that sent shivers down their spines.

"Let's go!" Cosmo cried.

They started scrambling back down the tree. "We'll travel monkey-style," Cosmo said, reaching for a vine. "It'll be faster." He gripped hold of the vine and swung on it.

"Good idea, Cosmo," Nuri called, following him.

Cosmo leaped from vine to vine through the jungle like a monkey, heading for the river and the starberry trees. Leaves brushed against him and smoke clouded his visor as he approached a grove of burning balloon bushes. He spoke to Nuri via his helmet's communicator: "If we want to stop Infernox, we're going to have to take the heat, Nuri. Swing fast!"

They raced over the top of the burning balloon-shaped plants, fire licking at their ankles. Cosmo's foot brushed one, and it exploded in a shower of red embers. Nuri blasted her flame-freezer downwards, trying to quench the flames.

Cosmo could barely see for smoke, but he could just make out the sound of the river up ahead. "We're getting close, Nuri!"

But as they emerged from the smoke, Cosmo suddenly felt a stinging pain in his shoulder. "Aaargh!" The pain shot through his body and he fell from the vine onto the jungle floor.

Wrapped around his arm was a yellow

snake with two heads. *A twin-snake!*
Cosmo saw fang holes in the shoulder of
the Quantum Mutation Suit. The snake
had bitten him! He shook it off and
shuddered with pain.

"Cosmo, what happened?" Nuri called,
jumping down beside him. She saw him
clutching his shoulder, and the snake

slithering away. She gasped, realizing the seriousness of the situation.

"It must have slithered onto me when I was swinging through the trees," Cosmo told her. He glanced at his shoulder. The fang holes in the suit were healing over, the suit's living mesh repairing itself, but it was too late: the snake's venom was already coursing through his veins.

"You need the antidote, Cosmo. Yellowbell pollen. Or you'll die."

Cosmo remembered what Brain-E had told him: that the bite of a twin-snake would bring about death within twenty minutes. "I know. But there isn't time to search for yellowbells," he said. "I have to fight Infernox now and save those starberry trees, or thousands of galactic citizens will die too."

"Then *I'll* look," Nuri said.

Cosmo raced off into the trees, trying to put the pain and fear from his mind.

He burst through the bushes onto the riverbank, where a row of shining starberry trees grew at the water's edge. And striding towards them was the enormous alien, Infernox.

The invader was over ten metres tall, with flaming red muscles that bulged and glowed, veined with molten lava. He was rolling a huge ball of fire in his hands, and the ground sizzled beneath his red-hot magma feet. He hurled the fireball at a starberry tree, making it burst into flames.

"Hey, leave those trees alone!" Cosmo shouted, sounding braver than he felt.

Infernox turned and saw him. "And who are you?" he roared.

"Cosmo Santos, G-Watch agent."

The alien laughed. "Ha! I will fry you!"

He hurled a fireball towards Cosmo – who leaped out of the way as it exploded behind him.

It was time to use the Quantum Mutation Suit. "SCAN," Cosmo said into his helmet's voice sensor. Images of aliens appeared on the visor's digital display as the Quantum Mutation Suit searched through its databank: an iron-shelled anvilon, a ten-clawed cortarg, a supersonic storm-hawk . . . Cosmo assessed their heights, weights and abilities. *Which could beat a firestarter?* he wondered. On the display appeared an image of a ferocious bear-like creature with a glowing hot body:

ALIEN: MAGMUS
SPECIES: LAVABEAR
ORIGIN: PLANET VULCANA
HEIGHT: 7.4 METRES
WEIGHT: 5.2 TONNES
FEATURE: VOLCANIC STRENGTH

Magmus the lavabear it is, Cosmo decided. He spoke into the helmet's voice sensor: "MUTATE!"

CHAPTER
SEVEN

TIME TO TRANSFORM

Cosmo felt his body tingle as the energy inside him activated the Quantum Mutation Suit. The tingling grew stronger, like electricity flowing through his veins. The mutation suit was fusing with the molecules of his body. He could feel his cells re-forming as his body grew larger and more muscular. His hands and feet turned into massive clawed paws and his jaw lengthened, filling with sharp teeth.

He felt himself heating up, glowing
red-hot like volcanic lava. He was
Magmus the lavabear!

He padded towards the invader and
snarled, "Prepare to be extinguished,
Infernox!"

Seeing him, Infernox took a step back. "What magic is this?" he said.

Cosmo felt strong. As Magmus, he scraped the ground with his paw, and with a burst of explosive power charged at Infernox. He shunted the red-hot invader backwards, tumbling him head over heels. As a lavabear, Cosmo was resistant to the heat. Infernox rose to his feet, but Cosmo swung his volcanic glowing paw and struck him hard on the chin.

Red-hot sparks flew from the invader's molten face and he roared with anger: "No one fights Infernox and lives!"

But Cosmo felt no fear. He took hold of Infernox, pinning his arms to his sides in a crushing bear hug. He squeezed tighter and tighter. A furnace was raging inside him, building pressure like a volcano. "Give up, Infernox!" he roared.

"Never!" the alien snarled. "I come on the orders of Kaos to destroy this planet!"

Cosmo held on with all his might, squeezing the invader, but his left arm and shoulder felt suddenly shaky – the venom from the twin-snake bite was starting to take effect. A wave of weakness washed over him and he felt his bear-strength failing. Suddenly flames blasted out of Infernox's body, hurling Cosmo backwards onto the ground.

"RESET," Cosmo said, and his lavabear body tingled as he turned back into a boy wearing the Quantum Mutation Suit. *I need that antidote fast*, he thought. He looked around for Nuri, but couldn't see her anywhere. "Nuri, where are you?" he said into his helmet's communicator.

"I'm still searching, Cosmo," came a crackly reply in his earpiece, as if she was almost out of range. "No sign of any yellowbells yet. Are you OK?"

But Cosmo didn't get a chance to reply. Infernox was striding towards him.

"I will destroy you and torch this planet!" the alien roared.

Cosmo staggered to his feet, weak from the venom but determined not to give up. "Oh no you won't!"

He summoned what strength he had left and shouted, "SCAN!" into the helmet's sensor. The Quantum Mutation Suit responded instantly. Images of aliens appeared on the visor's digital display: a sabre-toothed skreen-bird, a viper-headed whalax, a toxic tumon . . . He saw an image of a large lizard-like creature with scaly skin and a tail like a whip.

ALIEN: CHAMELAX
SPECIES: REPTILION
ORIGIN: PLANET KLOSS
LENGTH: 12.4 METRES
WEIGHT: 3.3 TONNES
FEATURE: ALL-TERRAIN CAMOUFLAGE

Camouflage will give me the advantage of surprise, Cosmo thought. *Chamelax it is*. "MUTATE!"

He felt his body tingling as its molecules began to mutate. He dropped onto all fours, growing bigger, with four muscular legs and a long whiptail. Scales covered his body – thick, tough scales like armour. He padded towards Infernox and they changed colour, to shades of green and yellow, camouflaging him against the bushes. He crawled stealthily along the river's edge.

"Furnace Face, over here," Cosmo hissed, a lizard's tongue flicking from his mouth.

Infernox was rolling a huge ball of fire. "Where did you vanish to?" he demanded, looking around.

Cosmo crept up behind him, his reptilion scales flashing with silver, camouflaging him among the sparkling starberry trees. As Chamelax, he blended with his surroundings perfectly. "I'm right behind you," he hissed. He swung his whiptail as fast as he could, lashing the invader hard.

Infernox roared with fury: "Argh!" He spun round, confused. "Show yourself!"

Cosmo whipped him again. "Can't you see me? Ha!" He ran round the invader as Infernox blasted flames off target. Cosmo lifted his tail high, ready to strike again, but suddenly it felt heavy, too heavy to swing – the venom from the twin-snake was weakening him again. Cosmo felt his strength leaving, the power inside him failing as the venom took hold. Chamelax's camouflage began to fade.

Infernox turned, glaring at him. "I see you now!"

The mighty fire alien shot a torrent of flames straight at Cosmo, blasting him back along the riverbank.

Cosmo's reptilion skin flashed different colours in the heat, then his whole body convulsed. The effects of the venom were worsening – Cosmo couldn't fight back.

"RESET!" he said, transforming himself back into a boy.

"There's no escape!" Infernox roared, hurling a fireball as Cosmo dived into the river for safety.

He ducked under the water, swimming to the bottom as another fireball exploded on the water's surface in a flash of orange. Looking up through his visor, he saw the looming flame-red figure of the invader staring down from the riverbank.

Now what? Cosmo thought desperately. The Quantum Mutation Suit was watertight but there was only a small amount of air in his helmet – it wouldn't last long. He felt his power draining away, as the venom in his bloodstream sent pain searing through his body. He could see the invader rolling another fireball. *I can't let Infernox win*, he thought. *The galaxy is relying on me. I have to fight. I have to!*

CHAPTER EIGHT

OVER THE EDGE

"SCAN," Cosmo said into the sensor of the Quantum Mutation Suit. On the visor of his helmet, images of aliens appeared once more.

My advantage is in staying underwater, he thought. *The fire alien clearly doesn't want to come in*. He had an idea, and selected an enormous underwater alien with ten long, gripping tentacles.

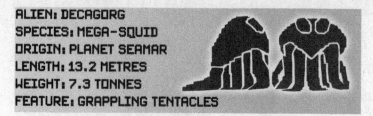

Cosmo summoned the last of his strength and yelled, "MUTATE!"

He felt a tingling again as the molecules in his body transformed. His body was becoming flexible. Ten long suckered tentacles pushed out of his sides, each as thick as a tree trunk. His flesh became see-through like a jellyfish, and feathery gills formed on his neck, enabling him to breathe underwater.

As Decagorg, Cosmo stealthily edged towards the riverbank where Infernox was standing. He saw the starberry trees burning beside the firestarter. Stretching out his tentacles, Cosmo pulled himself along the river bed, his huge body rippling in the current. His eyes were now on the top of his head, and

he could see the invader standing above
him. Infernox's body was pulsing red and
yellow, flames blazing from within.

"Are you hiding? Give up, do you? Ha ha ha!" Cosmo heard him roar. Infernox was laughing as though he'd already won.

Cosmo took a deep breath, his gills hungrily drinking in the water around him. Suddenly, from under the water, he shot up two long tentacles and grabbed hold of the invader's legs. His wet suckers steamed from Infernox's heat, but he didn't let go. Using all his mega-squid strength, Cosmo yanked hard, and Infernox splashed

into the water with a mighty hiss of steam.

"*Aargh!*" the invader roared.

The river bubbled, glowing fiery red. Cosmo wrapped his tentacles around Infernox, holding him down under the water, trying to extinguish his flames. The invader was struggling frantically, his red-hot body sending up clouds of steam. The water boiled as the two mighty aliens battled for supremacy. As they grappled underwater, they were being washed downstream by the current, faster and faster, bumping and scraping over boulders on the river bed.

I have to keep the fire alien submerged, Cosmo thought. But the venom was numbing his tentacles. The invader prised them off one by one, breaking free, and surged to the surface.

"I shall prevail!" Infernox roared.

All of a sudden, Cosmo heard a rumbling sound from up ahead. It was growing louder, and the air above the river was filling with spray. They were approaching a waterfall! Cosmo braced himself then, summoning all his power, grabbed hold of Infernox's leg and dragged him over the edge.

Down they fell, tumbling in a mass of tentacles and steam. With an almighty splash, they plunged into a lake below and were driven under by the weight of the water crashing on top of them. In the churning current Cosmo lost his grip on Infernox, rolling over and over before rising back up to the surface. The force of the current spat him out like a giant cork and, exhausted, he washed up in the lake's muddy shallows. Infernox appeared nearby, his massive body wrinkled and black, his fire almost out.

Cosmo tried to pull himself towards

the invader with his tentacles, but he had lost almost all his strength now. The struggle and the venom of the twin-snake were too much for him. Decagorg's tentacles were too heavy to lift.

Cosmo whispered, "RESET," and turned back into a boy wearing the Quantum Mutation Suit. His eyelids felt heavy, and images from his life flashed before him: places he'd been, things he'd done, his mother and father . . . His eyes closed – his life was slipping away.

But then, as if in a dream, a distant voice called to him: *Cosmo!* It was a voice he hadn't heard in a long time, the voice of his father. *Don't give up. The galaxy needs you. Use your power, Cosmo. Use your power.*

Deep within him, Cosmo felt a strength resisting his fate, a courage that wouldn't give in. He opened one eye and saw Infernox rising to his feet, now glowing a dull red and growing brighter every second. "I'm not finished yet!" the invader roared.

Neither am I! Cosmo thought, taking strength from his father's voice. With a supreme effort, he clambered to his feet, feeling the power flowing through him again. The Quantum Mutation Suit began to glow. *"The power of the universe is in me!"* he yelled.

A sword of white and blue light extended from Cosmo's gloved hand like lightning. He'd seen it only once before, when he'd defeated the first invader, Rockhead. It was the power sword, the power of the universe within him taking the form of a weapon.

"Time to leave the galaxy, Infernox," he ordered.

"Never!" Infernox bore down on Cosmo, fire burning in his eyes, about to blast him. Cosmo thrust the power sword upwards.

For a few moments his power and the invader's wrath were locked in battle. Every molecule in Cosmo's body was fighting for its life. He could feel power surging through him, extinguishing the invader's glow. Infernox roared and shook, convulsing and steaming. Then, all at once, he let out a cry of defeat: "*Aargh!*" His body hissed, and the alien evaporated into thin air.

"Good riddance, Infernox!" Cosmo said. He'd done it! He'd defeated the invader. He collapsed in a heap on the ground.

CHAPTER NINE

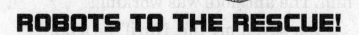

ROBOTS TO THE RESCUE!

"Cosmo! Cosmo, hold on!"

Through half-closed eyes, Cosmo saw Nuri clambering down vines beside the waterfall. She was calling to him, but he felt too weak to reply. She dropped to the ground and raced over, kneeling by his side.

"I did it, Nuri. I beat Infernox," he said weakly, but the venom from the twin-snake was now overpowering him, taking his life.

"I knew you'd win, Cosmo," she said.

Cosmo's vision was blurry. He could just make out Nuri holding a yellow bell-shaped flower.

"I found the antidote, Cosmo. It grows along the feeder streams upriver. I came as fast as I could." She gently opened Cosmo's mouth and shook the flower over it. Yellow pollen fell onto Cosmo's tongue. It fizzed, and after a few moments a warm strength began radiating through him. The antidote was working!

"You saved my life, Nuri!" he said.

"And you saved the galaxy from Infernox," she replied, smiling.

Cosmo sat up slowly, his strength returning, the venom nullified. "What about the other fires?" he asked.

Nuri pointed to Zaman's sky. Hundreds of harvester-bots were flying above the trees, sprinkling water from their hoses. "The harvester-bots are putting out the jungle fires. Brain-E gathered them all together."

Cosmo smiled. "Zaman's jungle and its medicinal plants are saved!"

He saw a harvester-bot coming down towards him with Brain-E dangling from it.

"Robots to the rescue!" the brainbot said, dropping to the ground beside him. "Master Cosmo, you beat Infernox. I knew you could do it!"

Cosmo blinked as Brain-E's lights flashed in celebration. "That invader won't be bothering the galaxy any more," he told it. "And Zaman will still be able to provide the galaxy with its vital medicines."

Nuri held out a helping hand to Cosmo. "Come on, let's get back to the Dragster," she said. "We'll radio G-Watch headquarters and tell G1 the good news."

Cosmo got to his feet, still feeling a little sore and light-headed, but now recovering from the fight and the effects of the venom.

Relieved to have succeeded in their mission, the trio headed off, triumphant.

***

Meanwhile, beyond the galaxy, in the cockpit of the battleship *Oblivion*, Kaos's five heads all stared at a blank monitor.

"What's happened to Infernox's navicom signal?" one head asked. "It was transmitting a moment ago."

"It's died! That's what's happened!" another head spat. "Infernox has failed."

"NOOOOO!" all the heads cried together. "He can't have!"

"He has!" hissed the first head.

Kaos marched up and down, his five heads muttering angrily. "So G-Watch has defeated the firestarter!" one head mumbled.

"And Zaman is saved – drat it!" another said bitterly. "What now?"

There was silence for a moment, then a little squeak came from the floor. The heads peered down and saw a purple rat licking its whiskers.

Kaos kicked it. "Well, don't just sit there, Wugrat!" he said. "Fetch me another navicom. It is time to unleash Zillah!"

All the heads cheered: "Zillah! Zillah! Zillah!"

Kaos hurried through the battleship to the cargo hold, where three huge aliens stood ready. "Step forward, Zillah," the outlaw said.

A huge fanged alien with spear-like limbs stepped from the group. "Zillah isss hungry," she hissed.

"Soon you shall feast to your heart's content," Kaos said, grinning. "Wugrat, hurry up!"

The purple rat scurried in carrying a crystal disc – a navicom transporter device. Kaos snatched it, turned its outer ring to set its coordinates, then reached up, attaching it to the alien. "Zillah, unleash

your terror," he said. "Destroy them!"

Zillah stalked into the centre of the hold on her long legs, then looked up as the roof slid open, revealing the swirling stars of the Doom Vortex. The navicom started to flash, and a blue light radiated from it. With a *whoosh*, Zillah shot up into space.

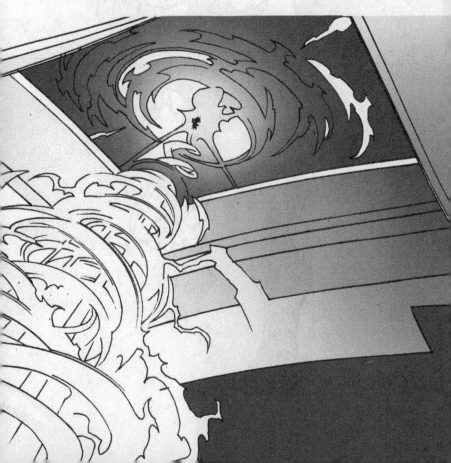

CHAPTER
TEN

DESTINATION: TRADEWAY

By the time Cosmo, Nuri and Brain-E
reached the Dragster, dusk was falling
over Zaman. Harvester-bots were
already busy rebuilding the laboratory.
Cosmo said goodbye to them and climbed
aboard the Dragster. He pressed a button
on the communications console and its
monitor flickered as it connected to
G-Watch headquarters. G1's face appeared
on the screen.

"Mission accomplished, G1," Cosmo said. "Infernox has been defeated."

The silver-eyed Chief of G-Watch smiled. "Congratulations, Cosmo," he said. "The galaxy is grateful to you. Its medicines are safe once again."

"Thanks, G1," Cosmo replied. "I couldn't have done it without Agent Nuri and Brain-E."

The brainbot flashed from the control desk and Nuri looked over from the co-pilot's seat, grinning. "Cosmo was ace, G1."

G1 looked at them gravely. "You have been exceptional, but your battles are not over yet. Our scanners have just detected a new invader beaming towards one of the galaxy's trade routes – the Great Western Tradeway. We believe it to be the fanged alien, Zillah – she must be stopped."

"We're on our way," Cosmo said.

"Good luck, team." The screen flickered as the transmission ended.

"Here we go again," Nuri said.

Cosmo started the Dragster's thrusters, then pulled back the throttle and blasted into the sky. He glanced down over Zaman's jungle – it seemed a happier place without the threat of Infernox: a herd of hogohons were grazing in a clearing again and a squadron of flying harvester-bots were waving goodbye.

Cosmo glanced at Nuri and smiled. "Set a course for the Great Western Tradeway. Let's go get Zillah!"

Join Cosmo on his next **ALIEN INVADERS**
mission. He must face – and defeat

ZILLAH
THE FANGED PREDATOR

INVADER ALERT!

Aboard space station *Orpheus*, Captain Provix kept watch as a convoy of eight cargo freighters approached along the Great Western Tradeway. The freighters were heading towards a vast zone of swirling asteroids: the Tarn Asteroid Belt. Provix reached out his webbed hand, switching on the space station's communicator. "*Orpheus* to convoy. I have a visual on you. Please reduce engine speed now."

"Instruction received," came the reply. "This is Convoy Leader Fortuna. How are conditions today? Are we in for a bumpy ride?"

Captain Provix pressed a sequence of buttons on the space station's control desk, activating its satellite receivers and deep-space imaging equipment. "The Tarn Asteroid Belt is experiencing erratic storms," he replied. "But *Orpheus* will guide you safely through. Sit back and relax. I'm locking on to you now."

The station's transmitters whirred as its supercomputer took control of the freighters' navigation consoles, overriding them and reprogramming their course.

Space station *Orpheus* was an advanced navigation station that monitored conditions in the Tarn Asteroid Belt, a wild zone of swirling rocks, debris and space dust that intersected the Great Western Tradeway. The area was a major danger to freighters trying to make essential galactic deliveries, and only *Orpheus* could guide them safely through.

Captain Provix had worked on *Orpheus* for six Tarn years. He was an experienced navigator from the distant planet Pialor, and his solitary temperament was well-suited to long periods spent alone in deep space. He watched from the control room as *Orpheus* remotely steered the eight freighters safely between moving asteroids, directing them on their journey through the Tarn Belt. He entered the convoy's details into the computer's log:

CONVOY: 10786956
COMPRISED OF: 8 DUCANOID FREIGHTERS
CARGO: GRAIN
DESTINATION: WESTERN WORL —

Suddenly the space station shuddered, throwing Captain Provix to the floor. *What was that – an asteroid hit?* he thought.

The emergency alarm sounded: *Whoop! Whoop! Whoop!*

Provix grabbed hold of the control desk, pulling himself up. Through the lookout sphere he saw *Orpheus*'s satellite dishes, antennae and probes spinning off into space. Warning lights were flashing on the control desk and the space station was rocking violently. Quickly he switched on the communicator. "Mayday! Mayday! This is Captain Provix requesting urgent help. Space station *Orpheus* is in trouble!"

He waited for a reply, but none came; the station's transmitters were down too. He heard a clawing and scratching sound coming from outside. *Something's attacking* Orpheus! he realized in terror.

Provix heard the station's metal hull being torn and wrenched apart. Suddenly there was a shrill hiss, and two long fangs pierced through the ceiling of the control room. Provix gasped. Green slime began oozing down the fangs, dripping onto the desk. It was some kind of chemical and the desk started to fizz and bubble, dissolving *Orpheus*'s supercomputer!

Captain Provix cowered, clinging to the

control panel as the metal ceiling tore open and a hideous face looked in – the face of a huge fanged alien with jet-black eyes.

"I am ZZZZZillah," the alien hissed. "And in the name of Kaosss I come to feed!"

CHAPTER ONE
TRADEWAY TROUBLE

"Hey, Nuri, what are you doing back there?" Cosmo called, as he blasted the Dragster 7000 spaceship away from the Dyad-24 star system, heading for the galaxy's Great Western Tradeway.

Agent Nuri, his blue-skinned co-pilot from Planet Etrusia, entered through the cockpit's interior door. "I've brought you something to eat," she said, handing him a pot of pink paste.

Cosmo looked at it, puzzled. "What is it?"

"It's space food from the supply cupboard," she told him.

"It looks revolting," Cosmo said, wrinkling his nose.

Brain-E, the ship's brainbot, bleeped from the Dragster's control desk and dipped its probe arm into the paste. "Master Cosmo, this contains precisely two thousand calories, plus protein, minerals and vitamins A, B, C, D, E, K and P. It's been specially designed in the G-Watch laboratory for deep-space missions."

Cosmo scooped out a blob of the pink

paste and swallowed it. "Mmmm, it's not bad," he said, surprised. It tasted like strawberry ice cream. He tucked in hungrily as the Dragster 7000 powered onwards, knowing he had to keep his strength up for what lay ahead.

Cosmo was an eleven-year-old Earthling boy on an urgent mission for the galaxy's security force, G-Watch. The evil outlaw, Kaos, had five fearsome alien invaders under his command, and was sending them to destroy the galaxy. Only Cosmo could protect it from their attack. Already he'd defeated two of them: Rockhead, the living mountain, and Infernox, the firestarter. Now he was trying to locate and fight the third invader: Zillah, the fanged predator.

"Nuri, could you select our course?" Cosmo asked.

"Right away," Nuri replied, programming the spaceship's navigation console. Details appeared on the spacescreen.

DESTINATION: GREAT WESTERN TRADEWAY, TARN JUNCTION
STAR SYSTEM: TARN ASTEROID BELT
ROUTE: HYPERWAY 7 JOINING TRADEWAY AT JUNCTION L2
DISTANCE: 2 BILLION MILES

Having eaten, Cosmo felt ready for adventure. He shot the Dragster between flashing space beacons onto Hyperway 7 then flicked the Dragster's hyperdrive switch; the stars in the spacescreen turned to bright streaks as he accelerated to twice the speed of light.

Nuri checked the course. "In two Earth minutes we'll reach Junction L2 of the Great Western Tradeway."

"What is this tradeway, anyway?" Cosmo asked.

"It's an essential route for spaceships travelling through the galaxy's Delta Quadrant," Nuri explained. "All kinds of freighters use it to trade supplies between the planets."

And now there's a fearsome alien on it, Cosmo thought. *Not good.* As they approached Junction L2, he switched out of hyperdrive and veered onto the Great Western Tradeway. He swerved to pass a slow-moving cargo ship then zipped by a line of livestock transporters. The tradeway was busy with space traffic; there were high-security ships transporting galactic gold and thick-hulled freighter vessels carrying food supplies.

Nuri glanced up from the navigation console. "G-Watch's scanners detected the invader beaming in near the Tarn Junction, where the tradeway enters the Tarn Asteroid Belt."

"Brain-E, what do you know about this invader?" Cosmo asked.

The ship's brainbot bleeped. "Well, according to my databank, Zillah is a female predator from the Doom Vortex; a scavenger who feeds on space wreckage in the vortex's treacherous storm zones."

"A scavenger that eats spaceships!" Cosmo said, shocked. "I don't want to end up as some freaky alien's lunch."

"Cosmo, slow down!" Nuri said.

Ahead of them was a space traffic jam: hundreds of ships were stuck on the tradeway. Cosmo reduced power. *What's going on?* he wondered. He weaved the Dragster between the ships, trying to find out. They were bottle-necked on the edge of a vast mass of swirling asteroids. On the spacescreen, the star plotter lit up, highlighting the asteroids, and a flashing red message appeared: DANGER! TARN

"This is weird," Nuri commented. "*Orpheus* should be guiding these ships through. There shouldn't be any jam."

"What's *Orpheus*?" Cosmo asked, flying carefully between two cargo carriers.

"It's a navigation station. It should be close by."

Cosmo peered nervously through the spacescreen sensing that something was wrong. "Nuri, over there!" he said, spotting a mangled silver structure floating on the edge of the asteroid belt. "Is that *Orpheus*?"

Nuri looked to where Cosmo was pointing. "Yes! What's happened to it?"

Cosmo steered towards the space station, shining the Dragster's searchlights. *Orpheus* looked broken and twisted. The bent remains of antennae and satellites were hanging off it.

"It's been attacked," Cosmo said. "Zillah must have struck already!"

The beam of the Dragster's searchlights illuminated someone floating in *Orpheus*'s control room – a wolf-headed man wearing an emergency oxygen mask.

"Look, someone's inside," Cosmo said.
"And he's in trouble. He needs our help!"

Find out what happens in
ZILLAH – THE FANGED PREDATOR . . .